BUZZ! BUZZ!

A FIREFLY BOOK

Published by Firefly Books Ltd. 2015

Illustrations copyright © 2014 Mango Jeunesse, Paris
English translation copyright © 2015 Firefly Books

First printing

Publisher Cataloging-in-Publication Data (U.S.)

A CIP record for this title is available from the Library of Congress

Library and Archives Canada Cataloguing in Publication

A CIP record for this title is available from Library and Archives Canada

Published in the United States by
Firefly Books (U.S.) Inc.
P.O. Box 1338, Ellicott Station
Buffalo, New York 14205

Published in Canada by
Firefly Books Ltd.
50 Staples Avenue, Unit 1
Richmond Hill, Ontario L4B 0A7

Printed in China

MEGA★WOLF

SÉVERINE VIDAL

BARROUX

How Mega Wolf saved
the little girl in red

FIREFLY BOOKS

Mega Wolf is big,
very big.
To see him fully,
you have to back up.

Further...

...further.

He is a magnificent wolf, as you can see.
He exercises many times a day.

1000 lbs

mega soft fur

You have to be in shape
to save the world!

In the morning, Mega Wolf loves to take a hot shower.

He also likes:

eating Little Red Riding Hood cereal,

checking out his muscles in the mirror,

pleasing the chick

He lives there, above the luxury car store
(and that works out well for Mega Wolf since he loves cars)!

Mega Wolf has the most beautiful, reddest shiniest sports car ever.

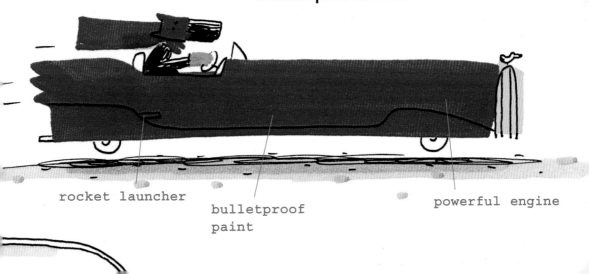

rocket launcher

bulletproof paint

powerful engine

In his Mega car, Mega Wolf is faster than the speed of light.

HURRAY!

In short, let's say that Mega Wolf is strong, muscular, courageous and very famous. Everyone admires him and screams "Hurray!" when he goes by.

He is extremely successful. And that's very normal, since Mega Wolf sometimes does unbelievable things.

Today, Little Red Riding Hood is going for a walk.
Her mother gives her the same advice she does every day.

Be careful! Beware of
the Big Wicked....

Yes, I know!
Of the Big Wicked
Mosquito!

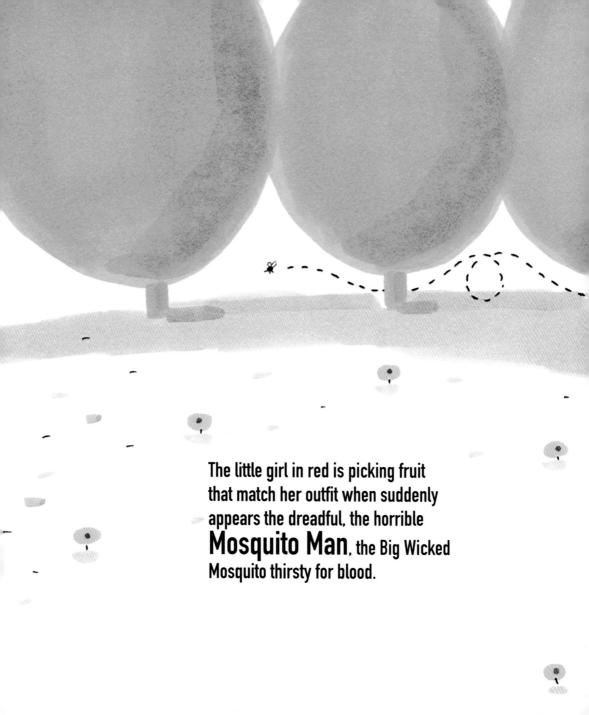

The little girl in red is picking fruit
that match her outfit when suddenly
appears the dreadful, the horrible
Mosquito Man, the Big Wicked
Mosquito thirsty for blood.

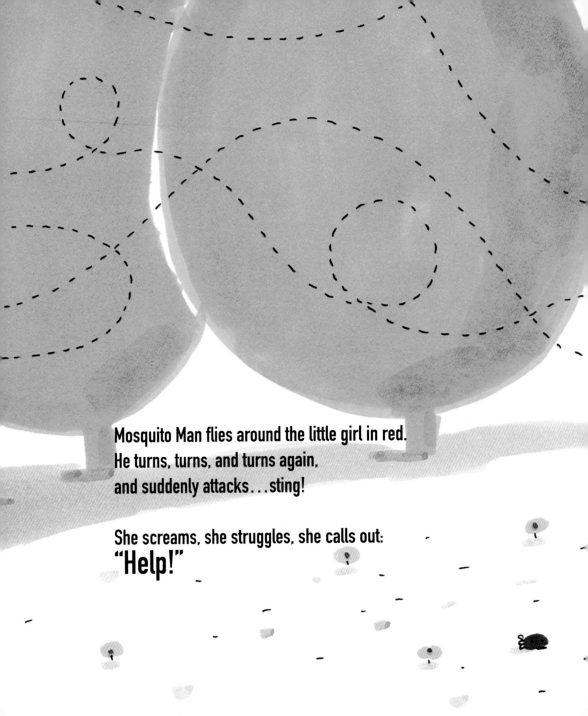

Mosquito Man flies around the little girl in red.
He turns, turns, and turns again,
and suddenly attacks...sting!

She screams, she struggles, she calls out:
"Help!"

Mosquito Man is very, very mean,
especially when he is very, very hungry.
And at this instant, he is craving a delicious snack.

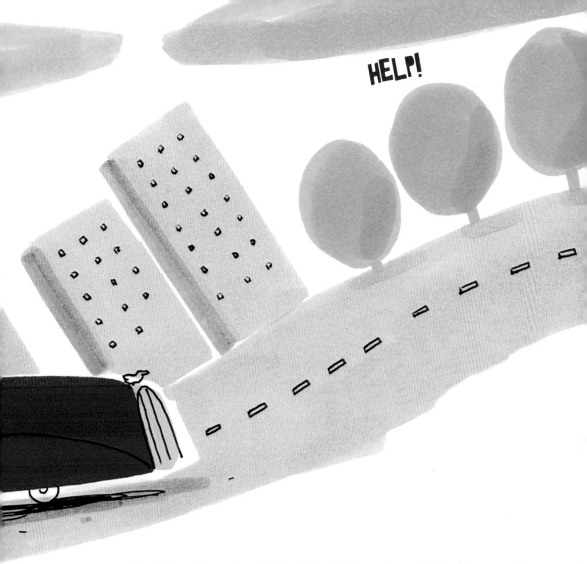

Just then, the cries of the little girl in red reach the big ears of Mega Wolf.
He jumps into his Megamobile and takes off with a bang.
The entire city stops in its tracks to let him drive by.

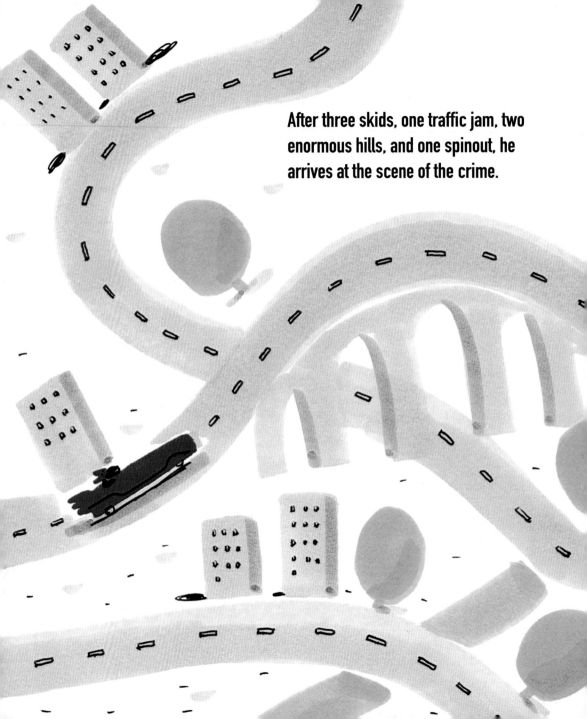

After three skids, one traffic jam, two enormous hills, and one spinout, he arrives at the scene of the crime.

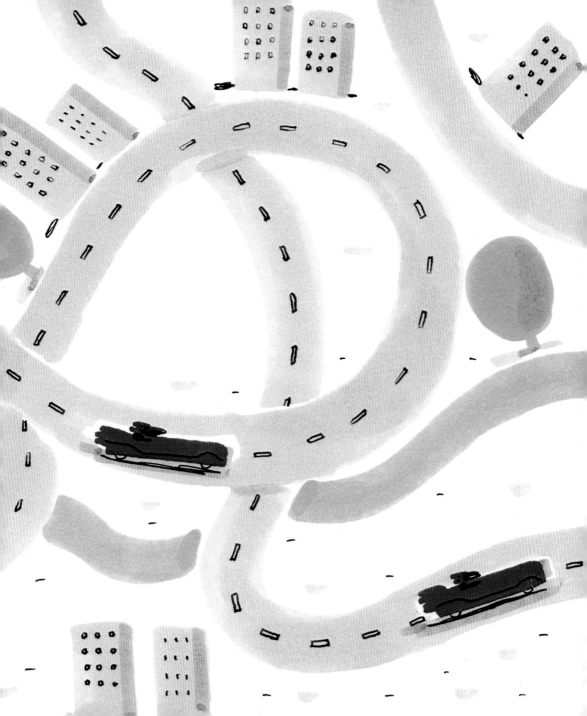

Mega Wolf doesn't hesitate to battle the dreadful and horrible Mosquito Man to save the little girl in red.

Mega Wolf has won the fight.

I'll be back!

Mega Wolf isn't afraid of anything, or anyone.
He does not fear Mosquito Man, or any other
frightful, dreadful, nasty creatures.
He is fast, strong and courageous.

But when he goes to sleep at night, after his day as a super hero...
It's with his teddy in his arms.

Shhh...it's a secret!

MEGA BEAR

MOSQUITO MAN

MEGA PIG

MEGA CROC

MEGA PANDA

MEGA HIPPO